Bramble the Hedgehog

To my grandpuppy,
Dutch — J.C.

Text copyright © 2018 by Jane Clarke and Oxford University Press
Illustrations copyright © 2018 by Oxford University Press

All rights reserved. Published by Scholastic Inc., 557 Broadway, New York,
NY 10012, *Publishers since 1920*. SCHOLASTIC and associated logos are
trademarks and/or registered trademarks of Scholastic Inc. Published
by arrangement with Oxford University Press. Series created
by Oxford University Press.

First published in the United Kingdom in 2018 by Oxford University Press,
Great Clarendon Street, Oxford, OX2 6DP.

ISBN 978-1-338-20025-6

10 9 8 7 6 5 4 3 2 1   18 19 20 21 22

Printed in the U.S.A.   23
First printing 2018

Book design by Mary Claire Cruz and Baily Crawford

Dr.KittyCat

Bramble the Hedgehog

Jane Clarke

Scholastic Inc.

Chapter One

"Peanut?" Dr. KittyCat meowed.
"Where are you?"

The floor of Dr. KittyCat's clinic was piled high with cardboard boxes stamped MEDICAL SUPPLIES.

But there was no sign of Dr. KittyCat's mouse assistant.

A sudden, loud yelp came from the middle of the boxes.

"*Eek!*" It was Peanut. "I'm boxed in!" he squeaked.

"Don't panic, Peanut." Dr. KittyCat put her furry paws against a heavy box labeled COLD PACKS. She pushed with all her might until she had moved it far enough for Peanut to scramble out of the gap. His fur was ruffled up, and he was clutching a crumpled piece of paper with what looked like a list on it.

"All the medical supplies I ordered arrived at once!" Peanut showed Dr. KittyCat the delivery list. "There are boxes of toothbrushes and toothpaste, triangular bandages, stickers, paw-cleansing gel, wipes, and cotton gauze swabs, as well as cold packs and all sorts of medicines." He sighed. "All this will take forever to unpack."

"It's important that we check and put away all the medicines ourselves. But most of these supplies are quite safe for anyone to handle," Dr. KittyCat said thoughtfully. "Call the school and ask if any little animals would like to come to the clinic at the end of the day to help unpack the supplies and put them away," she suggested. "We can take the volunteers to the carnival afterward as a reward."

"That's a great idea!" Peanut scrambled over the boxes to his desk. He picked up the handset of the telephone and dialed the number for Thistletown School. He twisted the cord around his arm and listened to the dial tone as he waited for someone at the school to pick up. *Ring . . . Ring . . . Ring . . .*

After school, the clinic was full of excited volunteers. All the little animals in Thistletown had come to help! Peanut scampered from box to box, checking things off his list and telling everyone where to put the supplies.

"These look fun," Posy the puppy woofed as she unpacked a box full of brightly colored toothbrush and toothpaste sets. "I'll need a new toothbrush when my grown-up teeth come in." She grinned, showing Peanut the gaps in her front teeth.

"I've already got my new teeth," Ginger the kitten meowed. She was heading for the stepladder with an armful of bandages.

MEDICAL
SUPPLIES

"So have I!" Logan gave a muffled yap. Peanut could only see his hairy tail. The rest of him was buried in the box of cold packs.

There was a chorus of "and me!" from lots of the other busy helpers.

Bramble the hedgehog gave a tiny, excited *squeeeak*.

"I have a wobbly tooth!" he said proudly. He put down the box of bandages he was carrying and scrambled up onto an unopened box. "Look, everyone! You can see it!" He opened his mouth wide and wiggled his front tooth with a claw.

"*Urgh!*" Sage the owlet shuddered.

"Don't force it," Dr. KittyCat
advised Bramble. "You'll make it sore.
If you leave it, it will just fall out—
probably when you're eating something
crunchy or chewy . . ."

"I never had baby teeth," Pumpkin said smugly. "Hamsters' teeth just grow and grow all the time. Like Peanut's."

"And ours!" said Nutmeg the guinea pig and Clover the bunny together.

"Birds don't need silly teeth," Sage hooted. "Beaks are best!"

"That's true," Willow the duckling agreed. "But I still clean my beak with a toothbrush every night and every morning," she quacked. "Don't you?"

There was a long silence. Peanut looked up from his checklist. Sage was ruffling her feathers.

"What's in here?" she hooted,
ripping at a big shallow box with
her claws. "It doesn't have a 'medical
supplies' stamp on it, or anything . . ."

Peanut peered in as she opened it.

"*Eek!*" he squeaked. The box was packed full of balls of wool in pale pink, dark green, and mustard yellow. Dr. KittyCat must have ordered more supplies for her knitting!

Beside him, Pumpkin gave a groan.

"I'm not sure I want Dr. KittyCat to knit me anything else, either," Peanut whispered to him sympathetically. "Especially not something that's the color of mustard!"

"It's not that," Pumpkin grunted. "It's this box of stickers. It needs to go on Dr. KittyCat's desk, but it's so-ooo-ooo heavy." He bent over the box and attempted to heave it up.

Dr. KittyCat appeared by his side. "Let me help with that, Pumpkin," she meowed. "I don't want you to hurt your back. If you ever have to lift something heavy on your own, you should bend your knees and keep your back straight," she went on. "When you're working, it's important to be careful . . ."

Crash! went the stepladder.

"*Yeowwwl!*" Ginger squealed. Peanut looked up from his checklist. The furry young kitten was dangling from a shelf by the tips of her claws!

Chapter Two

"Hold tight! You'll be safe in a whisker!" Dr. KittyCat meowed as she picked up the stepladder and put it up under Ginger's paws.

"Thanks. I was in a hurry to get all the bandages stacked on the shelf and I leaned over too far!" Ginger bounded down the stepladder and cheerfully

picked up another armful of bandages.
Peanut could see one of the packages
was broken. The end of a bandage was
trailing behind her. Before he could say
anything, the bandage wrapped itself
around Ginger's back legs and tripped
her. She fell on her bottom with a
bump.

"I'm OK," she said, springing to her feet.

Peanut and Dr. KittyCat looked at each other. Dr. KittyCat nodded, then stood up straight and clapped her paws. The little animals stopped what they were doing and turned to face her. "I'd like everyone to stop working for a moment and listen to a little talk about workplace safety," Dr. KittyCat announced. "Peanut, would you like to do it?"

"Ooh, yes!" Peanut climbed up the stepladder so everyone could see him. He held on tightly to the top and cleared his throat. He felt very important. "Slips, trips, and falls are the most common types of workplace accidents," he squeaked. "So clean up spills, don't leave things in the way, don't be in a hurry, and most of all—THINK SAFE AND BE CAREFUL!"

"Purr-fectly put, Peanut," Dr. KittyCat purred.

Peanut could feel his ears going pink with pride.

"You're doing a very good job, everyone," Dr. KittyCat went on. "Thank you all for coming to help. Keep going, but please remember to think safe—and be careful. We're almost done!"

Peanut helped supervise, and soon all the boxes were empty. Logan and Posy jumped up and down on them to flatten them out and stacked them up for recycling. Peanut smiled as he looked around. The clinic was back to normal. All the medical supplies were put away on the shelves and in the cabinets.

"Carnival time!" Dr. KittyCat announced.

"Yay!" the little animals cheered.

Dr. KittyCat picked up her flowery doctor's bag. "I need to put some of these new medical supplies in my bag," she told Peanut. "And make up my mind as to which lovely new ball of wool to choose for my next project . . ."

Please don't let it be mustard if it's for me, Peanut thought as he handed her the *Furry First-aid Book*. "Can you put this in your bag as well, please?" he asked. "I'm afraid I might lose it at the carnival!"

"It's very important to keep our patients' records safe," Dr. KittyCat agreed. "I'll go and see if I can fit everyone in the vanbulance . . ."

As Peanut made his way outside, he could hear Dr. KittyCat murmuring to herself as she checked the contents of her bag: "Stethoscope, ophthalmoscope, magnifying glass, tweezers, tongue depressors, ear thermometer, scissors, syringes, surgical head lamp, dental instruments, paw-cleansing gel, wipes, bandages, tape, cotton gauze, instant cold packs, peppermint throat drops, medicines, ointments, clinical waste bags, reward stickers . . . and a ball of lovely mustard wool!"

Peanut stood next to the flowery
vanbulance as the excited little animals
piled in.

"Make sure you fasten your seat
belts," he told them.

There was some squeaking and

meowing and woofing, then a whole lot of whimpering. Posy jumped back out. Her ears and her tail were drooping.

"There's a seat belt, but there's no room on the seat for me!" she howled. "I won't be able to go to the carnival!"

"Don't panic, Posy," Peanut told her. He went to investigate.

"There's just enough room for a little mouse like me," he reported back. "You can have my spot and sit at the front next to Dr. KittyCat. You'll need to adjust my seat belt . . ."

"Yippeee!" Posy chased her tail around and around in a circle for joy.

Peanut held the passenger door

open so she could leap up onto the front seat.

Then he scrambled into the back of the vanbulance and pulled the door shut. He squeezed onto the bench between Clover and Daisy and strapped himself in. The vanbulance wobbled slightly as Dr. KittyCat jumped in, and he felt a bump, which had to be her throwing in her flowery doctor's bag. It was followed by a bit of scuffling. *That must be Posy adjusting my seat belt around her tummy,* he thought. The front doors banged shut.

"Ready to roll?" Dr. KittyCat called.

"Ready to roll!" Peanut and the little animals yelled back.

"I can't wait to get to the carnival!"
Willow quacked.

Vroom! went the engine, and
the vanbulance sped off through
Thistletown, bump-bump-bumping
over Timber Bridge.

Peanut and the little animals in the back leaned to one side as the vanbulance rounded a corner.

"Duckpond Bend doesn't seem half as scary when I'm in the back," Peanut commented. "From here, I can't see how fast Dr. KittyCat's driving!"

"I like fast and scary rides," Ginger meowed. "I can't wait to go on a scary ride at the carnival. I hope I'm tall enough to go on the roller coaster!"

"The first thing I'm going to do is eat a candy apple," Bramble told them excitedly. "Dr. KittyCat says my tooth will fall out when I eat something crunchy or chewy, and a candy apple's crunchy AND chewy!"

"Er," Peanut squeaked. "I'm not sure that's what Dr. KittyCat meant . . ." he began to explain, but everyone was talking in the vanbulance. No one seemed to be listening to him.

"If that doesn't work, Bramble

could try licorice," Daisy suggested helpfully.

"Or a stick of rock candy," Logan chipped in. "That's my favorite."

"Nut brittle!" Nutmeg said excitedly. "Carnivals always have that. It's yummy."

There was a squeal of brakes, and the front doors of the vanbulance clicked open and banged shut.

"We're here!" Dr. KittyCat meowed, throwing open the back doors of the vanbulance so everyone could pile out. "Remember to think safe and be careful—and have lots of fun!"

Chapter
Three

Peanut gripped the merry-go-round horse's mane tightly as it gently rose and fell in time with the happy music. *This is exciting!* he thought. *And I didn't think I'd like going around and around at the same time as going up and down . . .*

"This is fun," Dr. KittyCat meowed from the seat behind him. Peanut turned around to look. She'd left her flowery doctor's bag in the vanbulance, so she had her front paws free. She was hanging on to the merry-go-round pole with one paw and waving at passing animals with the other. "But it's not very exciting. I think I'll go on the roller coaster next. How about you, Peanut?"

Dr. KittyCat is a bit of a daredevil, Peanut thought. Aloud, he said, "I'm too small for the roller coaster. I think I'll try the bouncy castle next."

"Think safe, be careful, and have fun!" Dr. KittyCat meowed. As soon as the ride stopped, she jumped off and headed toward the tall roller coaster. Peanut stood and watched for a moment. He could see the roller coaster cars at the very top. The little animals who were sitting in them suddenly waved their arms in the air and screamed as it dropped down the other side. The next instant they were upside down, looping the loop!

Peanut shuddered. *Dr. KittyCat is going to love that,* he thought as he made his way past the sweet treats stand to the inflatable rubber castle. It was jam-packed with excited little animals jumping up and down.

This bouncy castle's a bit too busy for a small mouse, Peanut thought. It made his tummy feel a bit panicky to look at it. Peanut gazed around the carnival field for something else to go on. The teacups and saucers looked fun, but maybe a bit tame, even for him. He liked the look of the pedal-powered cars, too—but maybe he was a bit too old for them . . . In the far corner, there was a Ferris wheel. The top of it was almost as high as the roller coaster, but the little pods were going around nice and slowly, and they were covered in mesh so that no one could fall out. *Maybe I'll go on the big wheel next . . . It looks nice and safe.* Peanut was still thinking about it when Ginger the kitten slunk over to his side. Her whiskers were quivering.

"They kicked me out of the bouncy castle for bouncing off the walls with my claws out," she wailed. "And I'm too small for the roller coaster, so I can't go on that, either. It's not fair!"

"Cheer up," Peanut told her. "See the big wheel over there? Would you like to come on it with me?"

"Yes, please!" Ginger meowed, cheering up.

Peanut and Ginger wove their way through the stands toward the Ferris wheel. They waved to Clover and Willow, who were busy trying to hook a rubber duck, and Logan, who was holding a stick of cotton candy and attempting to lick a strand of it off his nose.

There was a bit of a line at the big wheel, but soon it was Peanut's and Ginger's turn to step into a pod. The door gave an automatic click as it locked, and in an instant they were off.

"I've never been this high before!" Ginger giggled.

"*Eek!*" Peanut squeaked. He could feel the pod swaying, and it was making his tummy churn. He put his paws over his eyes.

"Look! I can see Dr. KittyCat on the roller coaster," Ginger squealed. Peanut peeked between his paws. Sure enough, there was Dr. KittyCat with a big smile on her face, holding her silver paws in the air as the ride plummeted down.

"This is fun!" Ginger meowed happily as the pod stopped at the top. It swung gently backward and forward in the breeze.

This isn't as scary as Dr. KittyCat's driving, he told himself. *There's no need to panic.* Peanut took a few deep breaths, and his tummy stopped churning. He was beginning to feel quite brave. He took his paws away from his eyes and looked around.

"Wow!" he squeaked. "You can see right across Thistletown from up here. I can see the duck pond, and the school, and I think that's the clinic over there . . ."

The pod gave a sudden lurch as the

ride started to descend.

"*Eek!*" Peanut gasped, clutching the seat with his paws. His heart felt as if it had jumped into his mouth. He stifled another *eek!* and closed his eyes. *Keep calm and think of cheese*, he told himself as he breathed slowly in and out. Cheddar, Stilton, Gouda . . . He imagined nibbling at his favorite cheeses, and in no time at all, they were back on the ground.

The instant the automatic lock clicked open, Ginger rushed around to rejoin the line.

"Again!" she squealed. "Let's do it again!"

"No, thanks!" Peanut sat still for a moment, opened his eyes, and heaved a sigh of relief.

But something wasn't right. From the pod at the top, there was a panicky squeak.

Peanut got out and looked up, shading his eyes with his paws. It was Bramble and he looked scared. The little hedgehog was all alone in a pod.

Peanut raced to tell the ride attendant, but the attendant said there was nothing he could do until the pod was on the ground—except talk to Bramble through a megaphone.

"Don't be scared, Bramble," Peanut called through the megaphone. "Shut your eyes and think of your favorite thing. You'll soon be on solid ground again."

Above him, the squeaking turned into a whimpering. The whimpers got louder and louder as the pod with Bramble in it got closer. It seemed like a long time before Bramble's pod was at the bottom of the ride.

"You'll be all right now," Peanut said comfortingly as he took Bramble's paw and helped him out of the pod.

"*Snurrk, snuurk, snuurk*!" Bramble sniffed as he staggered off the ride. He pressed his paws to his tummy and began to wail.

"I bet it's motion sickness," Peanut reassured him. "It can make you feel really sick, but it doesn't last long."

47

He led the little hedgehog onto the grass. "Sit down for a minute until it passes."

But whatever was wrong with Bramble wasn't so easy to fix. After a couple of minutes, the little hedgehog was crying even louder than before.

Bramble's whole body shuddered as he gave a final loud "*snuuuuurk!*," clutched his tummy, and curled into a ball. All his prickles were quivering.

He should be getting better, but he's getting worse! Peanut thought anxiously. He knew he should reassure the patient, but it was hard to comfort a hedgehog who had curled into a ball.

"Don't worry, Bramble. I'll put out a call for Dr. KittyCat," Peanut whispered to the prickly ball, near where he thought Bramble's ear must be. He turned the setting on the megaphone to maximum and took a deep breath. *I can't panic,* he told himself again. *I need to put out an announcement that's loud and clear so that Dr. KittyCat knows where to come and rescue Bramble.*

Peanut put the megaphone to his mouth. "DR. KITTYCAT, PLEASE COME TO THE FERRIS WHEEL. IT'S AN EMERGENCY!" he called. "YOU'LL NEED YOUR FLOWERY DOCTOR'S BAG!"

He repeated the call two more times. Then he knelt down beside the quivering ball of prickles.

"Dr. KittyCat will be here in a whisker," he told Bramble. "You'll be safe in her paws."

Chapter Four

A thunder of little feet made the
grass vibrate. Peanut looked up. He
and Bramble were surrounded! All
the little animal friends had heard the
announcement and rushed to the scene.
They stood very quietly, whispering to
one another and looking concerned.
There was a shuffling noise as everyone

made room for Dr. KittyCat to get
through.

Peanut sighed with relief. She was
carrying her flowery doctor's bag—and
it looked even fuller and heavier than
usual. She was sure to have whatever
she needed to treat Bramble inside it!

He stepped aside so that Dr. KittyCat could kneel down beside the sick hedgehog.

"I'm sorry you're feeling so unwell, Bramble," she told him. "I'm here to make you better. But first, I need you to be a brave little hedgehog and uncurl. Do you think you could do that for me?"

Bramble's rubbery nose slowly poked out of the ball of prickles. He squeaked tiny hurt squeaks as he uncurled.

"Thank you, Bramble, that makes it much easier for me to examine you and prescribe the proper treatment,"

Dr. KittyCat purred. "Can you tell me where it hurts?"

Bramble gave a big sniff. "It's my tummy!" he squeaked.

Dr. KittyCat was encouraged by Bramble's answer: It told her that he was fully responsive and that his airway must be clear. "Do you have pain anywhere else?" Dr. KittyCat asked him.

"No-ooo," Bramble sniffled.

Dr. KittyCat wanted to know when the pain started and if anything made it better or worse. Bramble did his best to answer. "Did you fall and injure your tummy on anything at the carnival? Or did anything poke into it or bump it?" Dr. KittyCat asked.

Bramble slowly shook his head.

"That's good," Dr. KittyCat reassured him. "Now I'd like you to roll onto your back so I can examine your tummy properly. Will that be OK?" Dr. KittyCat asked him. "I'll be careful not to cause you any more pain."

Bramble nodded. He groaned as he lay down.

"Well done," Dr. KittyCat said calmly. "You're being very brave." She gently pressed the palms of her paws over Bramble's tummy.

It's lucky that hedgehogs don't have spines on their tummies! Peanut thought.

"Let me know if it feels at all tender to my touch," Dr. KittyCat told Bramble.

Bramble closed his eyes. Peanut watched his face closely. The little hedgehog didn't wince at all as Dr. KittyCat examined him.

"I can't feel any lumps or bumps," Dr. KittyCat murmured. "I checked your tummy all over and I can't find any tender spots, either. Now I need to see if your temperature is raised."

Dr. KittyCat's checking to see if the lining of his tummy is inflamed, Peanut thought. If he remembered right, that was called peritonitis. Peritonitis

could cause sudden
abdominal pain—and a
high fever . . . He opened
Dr. KittyCat's flowery doctor's
bag and took out the ear thermometer.

Dr. KittyCat thanked him with
a smile. She put the hygiene cover
on the ear thermometer, gently inserted
it into Bramble's ear, and waited for
the *beep beep beep*. Then she took
out the thermometer and held it up
to read.

"Your temperature's perfectly
normal for a hedgehog," Dr. KittyCat
meowed. She handed the thermometer
back to Peanut to clean and put away.

"You can sit up again, if you'd like to, Bramble," she said.

"*Uuurg!*" Bramble groaned as he sat up. "I feel sick. Up here." He patted the top of his stomach.

"Have you vomited recently?" Dr. KittyCat asked. "Or had to rush to the bathroom with diarrhea?" Bramble shook his head. "Then it's unlikely to be food poisoning." Dr. KittyCat thought for a moment. With a few more questions she found out that no one else in Bramble's family had been sick recently.

"Does your head ache at all?" she asked. "That can make you feel nauseous."

60

"Nooo," Bramble groaned.

"Did you feel dizzy when you got off the Ferris wheel? I felt a bit sick and dizzy when I got off the roller coaster," Dr. KittyCat confessed.

"Nooo," squeaked Bramble.

"I don't think there's anything seriously wrong with you, Bramble," Dr. KittyCat said reassuringly. "It's probably just indigestion. But before I prescribe any treatment, Peanut will just check your notes to be on the safe side."

Peanut pulled the *Furry First-aid Book* out of Dr. KittyCat's bag and began to leaf through the notes he had made in the book. "There's nothing in

Bramble's notes that would explain why he's feeling so sick now," he said slowly. "But it reminds me of something . . ." He reopened the book at the front. "I know! It reminds me of Posy! When Posy felt sick, she'd actually swallowed something she shouldn't have . . ."

"Well remembered, Peanut!"
Dr. KittyCat purred. She turned to
the prickly little hedgehog. "Bramble,
have you swallowed anything you
shouldn't have?" she asked. There was
a moment's pause before Bramble
shook his head.

"I'd better check inside your
mouth," Dr. KittyCat told him.
Peanut passed her a disposable tongue
depressor.

"I can't see anything lodged in your
throat," Dr. KittyCat said, "but your
teeth are very sticky and there are some
bits that look like pieces of nut stuck
between them."

Bramble started to wriggle. "*Gak, gak, gak,*" he gagged.

Dr. KittyCat quickly removed the tongue depressor.

"What have you been eating since we got to the carnival, Bramble?" Dr. KittyCat asked him.

"*Yuk, guk, guk,*" Bramble moaned.

"I saw him standing by the sweet treats stand. He was eating a candy apple," Sage hooted.

"I saw him wandering around with a big bag of licorice," Logan woofed. "He held it out so I could take one, and I noticed the bag was already more than half empty."

"When I saw him, he couldn't talk
properly because his mouth was full of
nut brittle," Clover said thoughtfully.
"He mumbled something about Dr.
KittyCat, his tooth falling out, and
having to crunch and chew."

"Oh dear," murmured Dr. KittyCat. "That's not what I meant him to eat at all."

"I saw him next to the duck-hooking stand, holding a stick of rock candy," Nutmeg piped up. "He probably ate that, too!"

Bramble staggered to his feet. His face suddenly went very pale. "I'm going to throw up," he groaned. Dr. KittyCat grabbed a paper bag and held it out to him.

"*Gak . . . gak . . . gak . . . bleeergh!*" Bramble vomited into the bag. Then he lay back down on the grass and closed his eyes.

Dr. KittyCat looked up at Peanut and the crowd of little animals. "I think we all know why Bramble's feeling so nauseous!" She sighed.

Chapter Five

"Poor Bramble. Throwing up is terrible." Peanut took the ball of mustard wool out of Dr. KittyCat's bag and used it to prop up the hedgehog's head and neck.

Bramble had curled
back up into a ball.

"Peanut, please
could you dispose of
this safely?" Dr. KittyCat
handed Peanut the full barf bag. Peanut
held it at paw's length and folded over
the top to seal it. Then, holding it as far
away from himself as possible, he walked
slowly over to the vanbulance and
dropped it into the clinical waste bin.

"Thank you!" Dr. KittyCat held out
the paw-cleansing gel. Peanut squirted
some on the palms of his paws, and
handed it back to Dr. KittyCat to do
the same. She rubbed her paws together

and then she returned the gel to her bag and took out a small bottle of water.

"You don't need any special medicine," she told Bramble. "And I don't think it's a good idea to give you a peppermint throat drop to suck on as that has sugar in it, and you've already had too much sugar today. Just take sips of water. It will help settle your stomach."

Bramble kept his eyes closed as he clutched the bottle and took tiny sips. His face began to return to its normal hedgehog color.

"Thanks! I'm feeling much better now that I've thrown up," he murmured.

"I'm so sorry if I confused you, Bramble," Dr. KittyCat meowed, raising her voice so everyone could hear. "When I said your tooth might come out when you were eating crunchy or chewy foods, I was actually talking about things like carrots and celery and apples, or even a tiny piece of chewy cheese!"

"Oh!" Bramble squeaked.

"Fruit and vegetables are healthy to eat," Dr. KittyCat went on, "unlike all the sugary sweets at the carnival! If you eat too much sugar, it can make you overweight and cause health problems when you're older. And it's really bad for your teeth. Your baby teeth and your adult teeth."

"Oh no!" Bramble wailed. "I ate bad stuff!"

"It's OK," Dr. KittyCat said reassuringly. "Once won't do you any harm. It's when you do it again and again and again that you cause health problems."

"But sugary things are yummy!" Posy woofed.

"They are delicious!" Dr. KittyCat agreed. "Sugary things are very hard to resist. That's why we all have to be careful not to eat or drink too many."

Bramble opened his eyes and sat up. "Oooh! My tooth feels a bit funny," he said, rubbing his jaw.

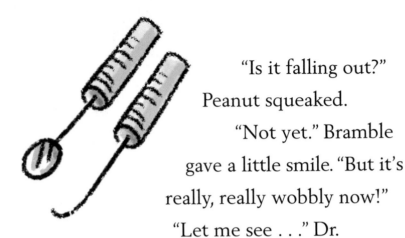

"Is it falling out?" Peanut squeaked.

"Not yet." Bramble gave a little smile. "But it's really, really wobbly now!"

"Let me see . . ." Dr. KittyCat reached into her bag and took out what looked like a small metal stick with a tiny hook on one end.

"Open wide!" she told Bramble. Bramble opened his mouth. Dr. KittyCat gently touched his front tooth with the dental probe. Even from where he was standing, Peanut could see that Bramble's front tooth was only holding on by a thread.

"Yes, your tooth is ready to come out!" Dr. KittyCat confirmed. She reached into her bulging flowery doctor's bag and took out a pair of surgical scissors. They looked very sharp as they glinted in the sunshine.

Bramble squeaked in alarm and jumped to his feet.

Chapter
Six

"Don't panic, Bramble," Peanut told
the little hedgehog. "It's just that your
prickles are tangled up in Dr. KittyCat's
knitting wool!"

"It'll take forever to untangle,
so I need to use my scissors to cut
you out," Dr. KittyCat explained as
she slowly and carefully snipped away

at the mustard wool.

Peanut took out a pair of long tweezers so he could pick off the short strands of wool without getting prickled.

"I'm sorry you won't be able to use this wool now," Peanut told Dr. KittyCat. "When I put it under Bramble's head, I wasn't thinking about your knitting . . ."

"You did the right thing, Peanut," Dr. KittyCat reassured him. "The comfort of our patients always has to come first," she meowed. "But this wool won't be wasted. I can use up all the short bits like this by making a lovely fringe around the bedspread I'm knitting for you."

Peanut opened and closed his mouth as Dr. KittyCat collected up the short lengths of wool and stuffed them back into her bag. He didn't know what to say. He was glad that he hadn't upset Dr. KittyCat. But, on the other hand, he wasn't at all sure that his bedroom needed a new bedspread, especially one with a mustard fringe . . .

At last he found his voice. "What else have you got in there?" he squeaked as Dr. KittyCat rummaged in her bulging bag and took out what looked like a tiny pencil case. She handed it to Peanut to open.

The little animals crowded around him so they could see.

"I know what it is," woofed Posy. "I unpacked a whole box of those!"

It was a bright blue toothbrush and a tiny tube of toothpaste.

"This one's for Bramble," Dr. KittyCat explained. "His baby tooth is ready to fall out and this should do the trick. Try brushing your teeth,

Bramble," she told him. "Be very gentle. It shouldn't hurt."

Bramble eagerly took the new toothbrush and squeezed on some paste. Then he slowly and carefully began to brush his front teeth.

"My tooth fell out!" Bramble squealed happily. He spat the tooth into his paw and looked at it. "There's only a tiny bit of blood on it, too!"

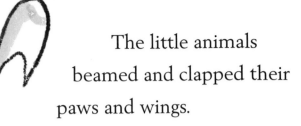 The little animals beamed and clapped their paws and wings.

"I have a little toothbrush and toothpaste kit in my bag for everyone," Dr. KittyCat said with a smile. "I packed them to give out at the end of the carnival trip to thank you for your help earlier. There are lots of different colors and sizes for you to choose from."

"Yay!" the little animals cheered.

"You'll all be able to give your teeth a good brushing when you get home," Dr. KittyCat told them.

"And I have a tooth to put under my pillow for the tooth fairy tonight!"

Bramble gave a happy gappy smile. "Please may I have a sticker, too?"

"We mustn't forget that," Dr. KittyCat purred as she handed Bramble a sticker. He stuck it on his tummy. It said "I was a purr-fect patient for Dr. KittyCat!"

"Thanks, Dr. KittyCat," Bramble squeaked. "You and Peanut are the best furry first-aiders ever!"

Peanut grinned from ear to ear. Tingles of happiness rushed from his whiskers to the tip of his tail. It was an even better

I was a purr-fect patient for Dr. KittyCat!

feeling than being at the top of the big wheel.

Dr. KittyCat closed her flowery doctor's bag. "Furry first-aiders are always happy to help," she purred.

The end

Dr. KittyCat loves brushing her teeth! Here are her top ten tips.

1. Always have an adult close by to help you.

2. Use a pea-sized blob of toothpaste.

3. Squeeze it carefully onto your toothbrush.

4. You should brush your teeth twice a day.

5. You should spend about two minutes brushing your teeth each time. An egg-timer can help you make sure you brush for long enough.

6. Use a mirror so that you can check where you are brushing.

7. Use small circular movements and brush gently.

8. Spit out any toothpaste when you have finished brushing.

9. Don't rinse your mouth too much after brushing.

10. Always clean your toothbrush by shaking it under running water when you've finished brushing.

Dr. KittyCat is ready to rescue Ginger the Kitten

Ginger was lying facedown on the grass, mewing pitifully. Her front paws were clamped over her nose. Mrs. Hazelnut was kneeling beside her, and the other little animals were gathered around, looking concerned.

"Dr. KittyCat's on her way!" Peanut panted.

"I think Ginger's hurt her nose," Mrs. Hazelnut whispered in his ear. "But I can't get her to take her paws away from her face so I can look at it."

"Dr. KittyCat will know what to do," Peanut said. "She asked us to get Ginger to the nature hut if we are sure she hasn't broken a bone."

A note from the author:

Jane says...

My grandpuppy Dutch chewed at everything with his tiny, pointy puppy teeth. One day, he tried to chew a hole through the hall wall. It's been filled in, but you can still see the dent!

See you next time!

Visit Friendship Forest, where animals can talk and magic exists!

Molly Twinkletail Runs Away

Ellie Featherbill All Alone

Bella Tabbytoe In Tree

Lucy Longwhiskers Gets Lost

Sophie Flufftail's Brave Plan

Emily Prickleback's Clever Idea

Ruby Fuzzybrush's Star Dance

Rosie Gigglepip Lucky Escape

Poppy Muddlepup's Daring Rescue

Special Edition!

Amelia Sparklepaw's Party Problem

Special Edition!

Meet best friends Jess and Lily and their adorable animal pals in this enchanting series from the creator of Rainbow Magic!

SCHOLASTIC

scholastic.com

MAGIC